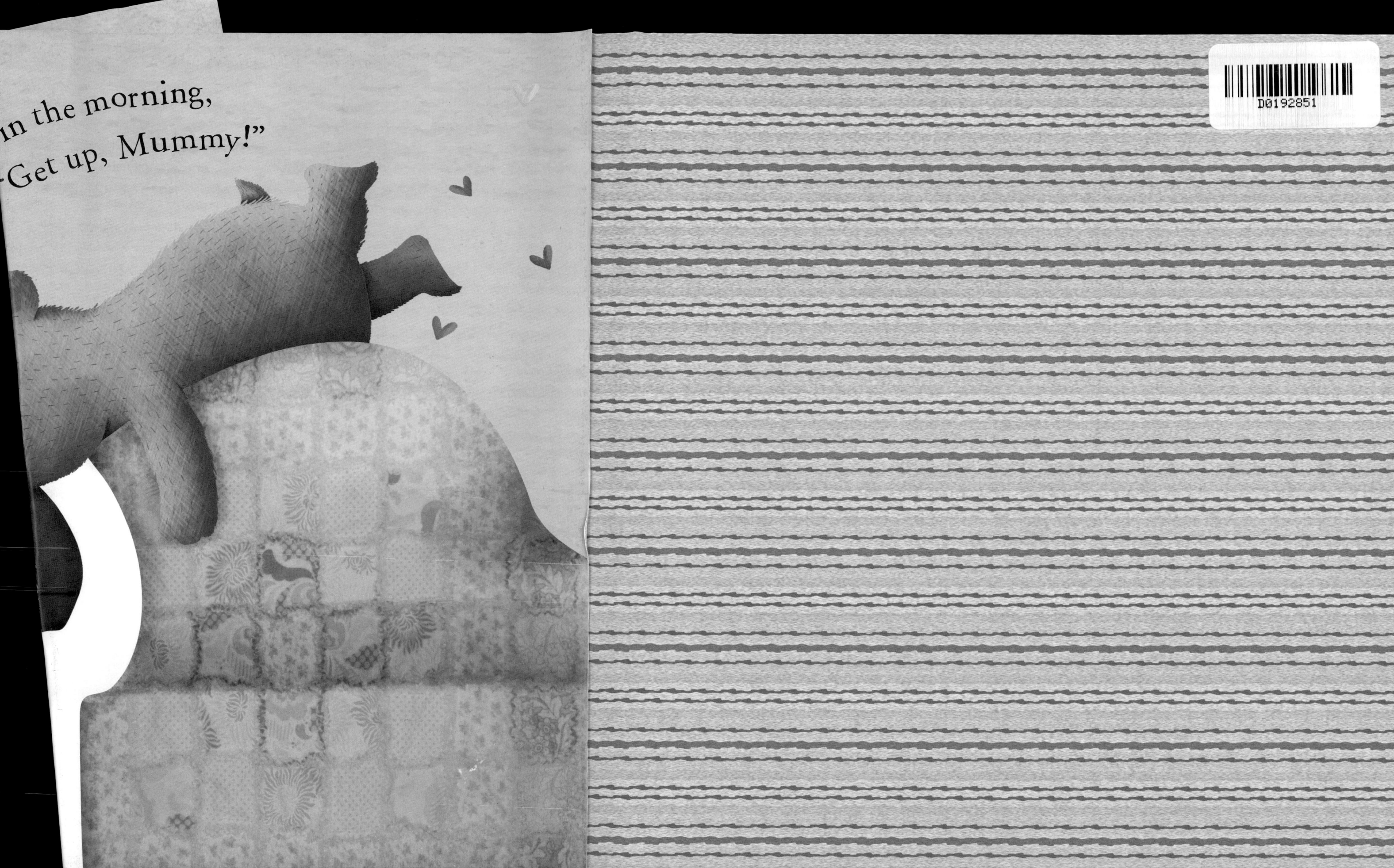

in the morning,

"Get up, Mummy!"

Kiss me

when I say,

Kiss me in the morning, when I say, "Get up, Mummy!"

Kiss Me

igloobooks

Kiss me
on my nose...

...and tickle me on my tummy.

Kiss me when you catch me,
as we play a game of chase.

Kiss me when you find me
in my special hiding place.

Kiss me when
I play my drum
and make
a lot of
noise!

Kiss me when I make a mess
with all my special toys.

Kiss me when I'm sad, so that you cheer me up.

Kiss me when I spill my drink
out of my yellow cup.

Kiss me
when my paintbrush
makes a rainbow splatter.

Kiss me and gently say,
"It really doesn't matter."

Kiss me when I cry because
my friends have all gone home.

Kiss me and tell me that
I will **never** be alone.

Kiss me when I am nervous
and I feel so very small.

Kiss me and hug me tight,
so that I feel ten feet tall!

Kiss me when the night-time comes
and scary shadows creep.

Kiss me when I'm very tired
and I am half asleep.

Kiss me so very gently...

... and rock me to and fro.

Kiss me and say, "I love you..."

... I'll never let you go."